THE DAILY QU[

HAWKEYE HAMILTON

BEAKY GARRILL

The Corrections Dept.

The corrections department would like to apologise for a typographical error in yesterday's issue. Readers were led to believe that the Bird-drain Bath Company could assist with pluming problems. This is not the case. We apolologise for any contusion clawed

Flaming O's
CANDLE
EMPORIUM

FOR MY GRANDAD
who loved detective stories,
my **sister** who likes them, **and my brother**
whose opinion remains a mystery.

Chloe   Jackson   Isla
Rayna   Ben

& JONNY

First published in Great Britain in 2017 by Andersen Press.,
20 VAUXHALL BRIDGE ROAD, LONDON SW1V 2SA

Copyright © Meg McLaren 2017

The right of Meg McLaren to be identified as the author and illustrator of this work has been asserted by her in accordance with the copyright, designs and patents act, 1988

BRITISH LIBRARY CATALOGUE IN PUBLICATION DATA AVAILABLE
ISBN 978 1 78344 483 0

CULTURE VULTURE

Your guide to this season's latest trends

Business was slow,
just the way I liked it.

PIGEON P.I.
TWO BEAKS ARE BETTER THAN ONE

CLOSED

MISSING
PET COCKATOO
"CURLY"
LAST SEEN AT HOME, ADMIRING HIS OWN REFLECTION
LIKES: MIRRORS, SHINY OBJECTS, SOFT FURNISHINGS
LOVES: HIS OWNER, MRS HIGGINS-SMYTHE
DISLIKES: THE GREAT OUTDOORS
IF SIGHTED PLEASE CALL 555-2513

My partner Stanley had
skipped town a while back,
so I'd decided to
take things easy.

Then the Kid showed up.

She'd been around for a while.

It was time to find out why.

She said she'd come to the city with friends, ready for adventure, but they'd found it a little too soon...

She'd had a narrow escape
but her friends hadn't
been so lucky.

MILK

MISSING
PET RUBINO BOURKE PARROT
"RUBY"
LAST SEEN IN HIS CAGE, OUTSIDE HER NEW HOME.
LIKES: MUNCHING
LOVES: NONE OF YOUR BUSINESS
DISLIKES: NEVER YOU MIND!
IF SIGHTED PLEASE CALL

MISSING
PET BUDGERIGAR
"JIMMY"
LAST SEEN IN HIS CAGE, OUTSIDE HIS
LIKES: GARDENING
LOVES: CROONERS, LIBRARY QUI
DISLIKES: LISTS
IF SIGHTED PLEASE CALL

No one had seen them since.

I told her I didn't take cases anymore.

But she was pretty convincing.

"Come back tomorrow and we'll talk," I said. But she didn't.

I didn't see her again for weeks.
When I finally did, it was too late.

The police were busy on a big case. I was going to have to do this alone.

News travels fast
in this town, especially
the bad kind.

Word on the wire
was that birds had been
going missing all over.

BIRDS
OF A FEATHER

BAKE
TOGETHER

A BEGINNER'S GUIDE TO
BIRD WATCHING

WOOD PIGEON

HOMING PIGEON

RACING PIGEON

HOUSE SPARROW

TREE SPARROW

LESSER-SEEN
BEACH SPARROW

COMMON GULL

HERRING GULL

SEAGULL

AHOY!

YOU WILL
NEED...

BINOCULARS

NOTEBOOK

PENCIL

NOM
NOM

MHMM

All the evidence
pointed to the
Red Herring
Bar and Grill.

It was time to take
a closer look.

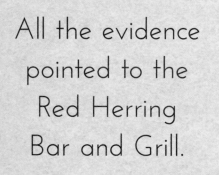

I was trying my best
to blend in...

AND STAY OUT!

Something someone didn't want me to see.

when something caught my eye.

I was in the right place,
I just needed to find another way inside.

It didn't take
me long.

And she
already had
a plan.

The Kid turned out to be a genius at picking locks.
Everything was going well until...

It was the infamous feather thief!
I couldn't leave now – I was so close to the truth.

As usual, my curiosity got the better of me.
Everyone else made it out safely,

but it looked like
my wings were
clipped for good.

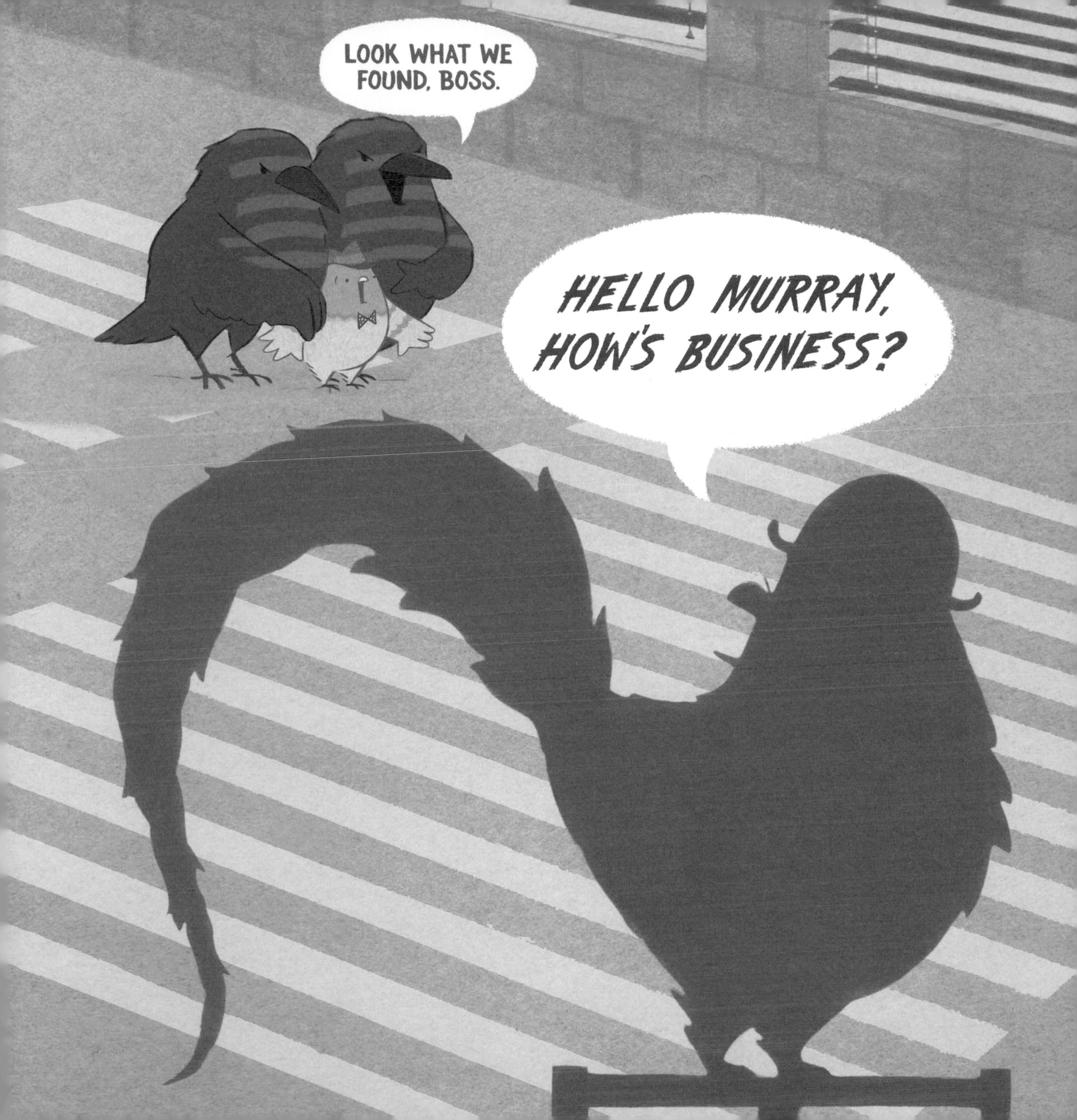
LOOK WHAT WE FOUND, BOSS.
HELLO MURRAY, HOW'S BUSINESS?

It was Stanley,
my old partner.

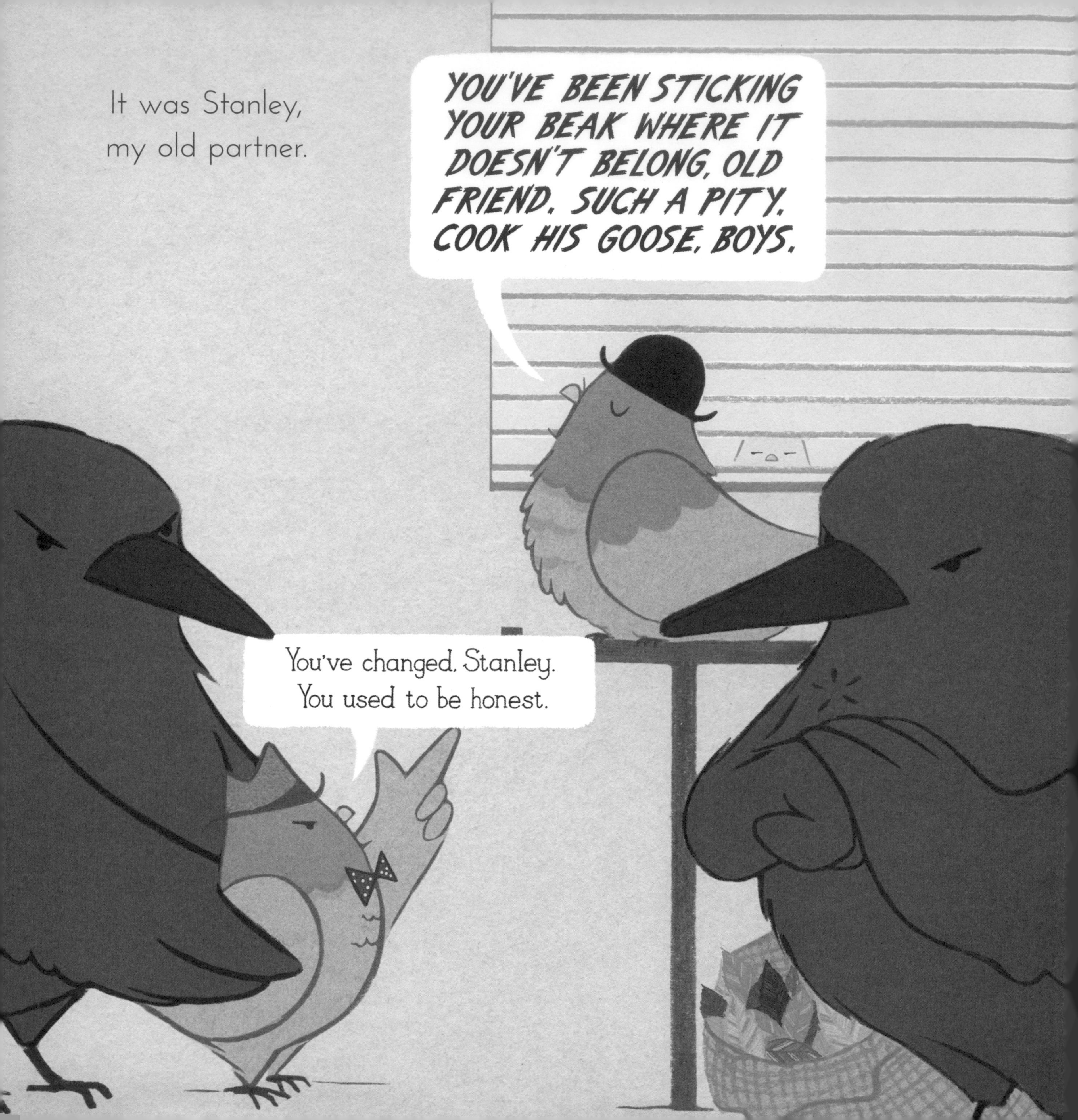

THESE HEAVIES
ARE HEAVIER
THAN THEY LOOK!

WHOOPS!

After all, that's what partners are for.

With another jailbird behind bars,
the streets were safe again
and I planned to keep
them that way.

SLURP!

The
EARLY
BiRD

SLURP!

OODLES OF NOODLES

With a little help, of course.

ADVANCED DETECTION